THE
REWARD

Diane Kay Larson
Illustrated by Emily Hagen

This is a work of fiction. All of the characters, names, incidents, organizations, and dialogue in this novel are either the products of the author's imagination or are used fictitiously

WestBow Press books may be ordered through booksellers or by contacting:

WestBow Press
A Division of Thomas Nelson & Zondervan
1663 Liberty Drive
Bloomington, IN 47403
www.westbowpress.com
844-714-3454

Interior Image Credit: Emily Hagen

Scriptures taken from the Holy Bible, New International Version®, NIV®. Copyright © 1973, 1978, 1984, 2011 by Biblica, Inc.™ Used by permission of Zondervan. All rights reserved worldwide. www.zondervan.com The "NIV" and "New International Version" are trademarks registered in the United States Patent and Trademark Office by Biblica, Inc.®

ISBN: 978-1-6642-3700-1 (sc)
ISBN: 978-1-6642-3701-8 (e)

Library of Congress Control Number: 2021911647

Print information available on the last page.

WestBow Press rev. date: 07/27/2021

WESTBOW
PRESS®
A DIVISION OF THOMAS NELSON
& ZONDERVAN

Acknowledgements

I would like to thank my husband Greg, who has read and given feedback to every version of the book as we revised it numerous times. Without his encouragement, this book would never have been possible.

Thank you and many blessings to Emily Hagen who illustrated the book and made the story come to life. Her unselfish talent is incredible. The first time we met we prayed together for the message in this book to become life-giving to many.

Above all, thanks be to God who gives us all good things.

This was the best day of my life! In all my eleven years, this was the best day of my whole life! My reward was more than I could have ever dreamed.

My name is Jimmy and I'm the oldest child in my family. I have two younger sisters who love to help our mom in the kitchen and in the garden. My mom is beautiful, and kind, and she has lots of friends.

We live in a small town by the Sea of Galilee in a house made from clay and straw and stones like our neighbors. We have small homes because Herod's taxes make it too expensive to have large homes.

My dad is big and strong. He is a net maker. All the fishermen in the area buy their nets from him because his nets are the best. Dad is teaching me to make nets too and I work with him every day. Dad makes big nets with strong cord for catching big fish and I make smaller nets that have smaller holes, so the small fish can't swim through them.

Dad has taught me to tie strong knots, so my lighter weight nets are strong enough to catch lots of small fish. I can see my hands getting stronger and more calloused from working with the cord every day, and I like how my hands are starting to look more like my dad's hands.

Yesterday, after I had finished my work, Dad said, "Jimmy, you have been so much help, tomorrow after breakfast, I'm going to give you a surprise as a reward for your hard work."

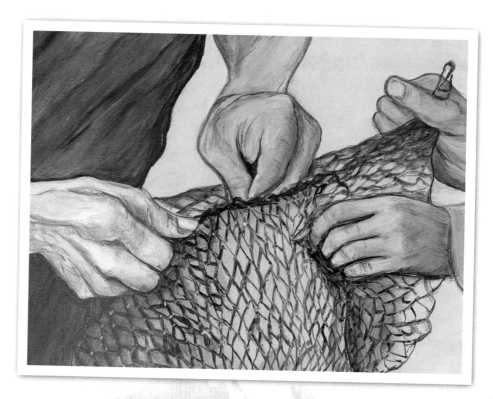

Finally, it was morning and at breakfast Dad said, "You know, Jimmy, you are getting to be a fine young man. You work hard and don't complain. We think you are old enough to take a trip on your own." I looked at Mom and she just smiled and handed me some breakfast of bread and cheese.

Wow! I almost couldn't believe it! My mom and dad think I am big enough to make this long trip by myself, to visit my cousins. I jumped up and hugged my dad and then my mom and gave her a kiss on her cheek!

"Thank you!" I said, and I ate my breakfast.

Dad went on to say, " I know you have wanted to visit your cousins Alex and Thomas, but since they live a half day's walk from here, we have not had the time to let you go for a visit because we were behind on our work. Now, because of your good work, we are caught up on our orders and even have some extra nets to display. Just remember as you go, like we have in the past, stay along the road by the sea all the way. Mom has packed a lunch for you." I took my basket with lunch in it and was on my way out the door.

Turning to wave good-bye, I found myself looking back at my house over and over until it was out of sight. I couldn't help but smile to myself as I thought of how grown-up I was now. Even Dad's words, "fine young man." He didn't call me a big boy; he called me a young man. I really felt like a "young man" walking the road all by myself.

As I was walking and feeling really happy with myself, I noticed there were lots of people on the road today. There were many more than usual, and they all were excited and in a hurry. It was so hot and dusty that I decided to walk over to the water and wash my feet and rest a minute.

While I was washing my feet in the water, a frog jumped out from a clump of grass.

I chased it for a minute and almost caught it, but it slipped through my fingers and got away. It swam under the water until it was out of sight. I tried to hold my breath until I could see it come up, but the frog was under water too long and I couldn't see where he came up, so I stopped holding my breath.

I looked down, and I found some pebbles and skipped some across the water. I was able to skip one seven times!

Suddenly, I noticed that the crowd grew louder. There was a crowd of people walking off the road over to the foot of the mountain. This was a REALLY big crowd and it was still growing! It looked like more people were coming from all directions and I was surprised that I hadn't noticed before that so many had gathered.

I put my sandals on and started walking along the road again.

As I was getting closer to the mountain area, I heard two men talking together saying, "I wonder if he will heal someone today." These men were so excited, I said, "Excuse me, who are you talking about?" they said, "Jesus! You're going to see him, aren't you?" I told them that I really had to get on my way to see my cousins, so I didn't have time today. I wished them well and hurried off.

I love to visit my cousins. They build furniture with their dad and when I visit, I get to help. Someday I might make some furniture for my family. I was excited to see what type of furniture they were working on now.

When I walked by the foot of the mountain, I saw the crowd was listening so intently that I decided to go over to find out what was so captivating. I got closer and could see they were all listening to that one man. I went even closer and I was surprised because it seemed like he was talking right to me. I asked someone who He was, and they told me His name was Jesus. So this was the man that the ones on the road were talking about.

I remembered I had heard some people that bought nets from my dad talk about Jesus too, and now I was seeing who everyone was talking about. Then I saw Andrew and his brother, Simon Peter, who had bought nets from my dad. I went over to them and they invited me to sit with them.

I sat still and listened as Jesus talked about heaven; how God sent Jesus from heaven to teach us more about God and provide a way for us to live safely with Him forever. I knew right then that I would love Jesus for the rest of my life. I wanted everyone to know Him! My dad sent me on a trip for a day, but God sent his Son to earth to teach us and save us forever.

I had been walking a long time before stopping to listen to Jesus. It was getting late into the afternoon and I was starting to get hungry. I opened my basket that Mom packed for me and saw she had packed fish and bread. Mom had carefully packed them in leaves and a napkin.

Andrew saw that I had some food and asked me, "Jimmy, would you come with me to see Jesus?" I didn't wait one second, I jumped up and went with him right away! Andrew showed me to Jesus and said, "Here is a boy with five small barley loaves and two small fish, but how far will they go among so many?" (John 6:9 NIV)

Andrew told me that the people were hungry, and that Jesus wanted my food to feed them. I looked at my food and thought abut keeping just one small loaf for myself because I was hungry, but when I looked at Jesus, I trusted Him and said, "Yes, He can have it all."

Jesus directed the men with Him to have the people sit down in the green grass. Jesus looked tired, but He had such loving eyes as He looked at everyone. Then Jesus took the loaves and looking up to heaven He gave thanks for them and the fish too.

Jesus broke them into pieces and had the food served to all the people that were there. We all ate until we were full, and I couldn't even eat all I took. So, Jesus told the men to pick up all the scraps and there were 12 baskets full. Andrew told me that there were about five thousand men along with women and children that were fed that day. Andrew explained to me that this was a miracle and Jesus is God's only son and has the power to do many miracles.

There was so much excitement, but it was getting late so Jesus asked people to leave and He went to get into a boat. I hugged Andrew and told him that I would never forget meeting Jesus. I thanked him for introducing me to Him.

I continued on my way to see my cousins. I wasn't thinking anymore about what a young "man" I was. All I could think about was the man I had just seen and how he had changed me. I kept running all these things through my head until I found myself at my cousins' house.

I called to them and Alex came running out of the house and shouted, "Jimmy! I'm so excited to see you! I must tell you about Jesus!"

I told him, "I just met Him! Jesus fed five thousand people today and did a miracle using only my lunch of five loaves of bread and two fish that Mom packed for me!" My cousins and aunt and uncle and I talked until late at night about all we had seen and heard about Jesus.

Now as I go to sleep and pull the blanket up around my neck, I look out the window at the stars and smile. This day that started with a reward from my parents became the best reward of all. Jesus did a miracle because I gave Him what I had. Now, my reward for believing in Jesus will result in eternal life in heaven! I don't think I will be able to sleep tonight because tomorrow it will be such joy to tell my family about this best day of my life and how we all can have the best reward of all. "Good night, Jesus, I love you."

End notes:

This book was inspired by the stories in the Bible of Jesus feeding the 5,000 found in Matthew 14:13-21, Mark 6:32-44, Luke 9:10-17 and John 6:1-13. I imagined what the story could be with the boy who had the loaves of bread and fish that Jesus used to preform that miracle. This tells that boy's story.

It is my prayer that this fictional story will reach many with an understanding of the rich reward that Jesus offers each of us.

Printed in the United States
by Baker & Taylor Publisher Services